Mel Bay Presents

A Treasury of Hymns
and Spirituals

for Autoharp,
Guitar, Ukulele, Mandolin, Banjo, and Keyboard

Compiled by Meg Peterson

Edited by Cary Santoro

Meg Peterson

Meg Peterson has written and arranged over thirty autoharp books. She has developed a leading teaching method, *Complete Method for Autoharp and Chromaharp* (93657), for all ages which takes the student from the simplest strumming to the most difficult picking styles. She has led workshops in schools and universities both in the United States and abroad for thirty-five years, and has been instrumental in the re-design and promotion of this popular instrument.

Cary Santoro

Cary Santoro taught general music in Connecticut for twenty six years, having trained extensively in Orff and Kodaly. The last sixteen years she was the music director at the Whitby School in Greenwich, CT where she worked with students aged 18 months through 9th grade. In this capacity she wrote and directed musicals, conducted courses, and coordinated an instrumental program. The autoharp was an integral part of her work with children.

1 2 3 4 5 6 7 8 9 0

Visit us on the Web at www.melbay.com — E-mail us at email@melbay.com

Preface

The hymns and spirituals in this book have been chosen because of their familiarity and popularity. They have been arranged in keys that are most suitable for singing, and can be played using only the words and the accompanying chords. In some cases there is more than one version of a particular tune. If both versions are well known, I have included both. If not, I have selected the one that is most widely used. These songs may be played on any instrument capable of chords, ie. guitar, banjo, ukulele, mandolin, keyboard, etc...

I have arranged the songs for the 15 and 21 chord standard Autoharp. Those who have diatonic or specially made instruments will be able to adapt the arrangements by transposing the melodies to a different key as explained in *Mel Bay's Complete Method for Autoharp or Chromaharp*.* The songs are also chorded for a variety of styles, from simple strumming (few chords) to melody picking (more frequent chord changes).* You can hear the melody emerge as you vary your stroke and play in the different areas (octaves) of the Autoharp.

A slash (/) means to repeat the chord in the rhythm of the song until a new chord is indicated. Slashes also indicate the rhythmic pattern of the piece. When there are several slashes over one word, the strokes will naturally be shorter and the tempo (speed) will be faster. These slashes can be varied and will help make your playing more interesting, whether it's accompaniment or a melody solo. You may add or subtract slashes as you perfect your own style. They are merely guidelines and need not be followed rigidly.

A quarter rest (𝄽) means that you do not sing on that beat. Sometimes you will stroke a chord on it, and other times you will remain silent.

A repeat sign (:‖) means to repeat the previous verse or phrase.

D.C. is an abbreviation for Da Capo, which means "from the beginning."

Fine means the end.

D.C. al Fine means to go back to the beginning of the song and play to *Fine*.

⁞ means *Arpeggiando*, * a slow, gentle stroke from the lower to the higher octave.

A chord is put in parentheses if it is not essential to the harmony, but just adds color to the arrangement. If you do not have that particular chord on your Autoharp, just continue playing the previous one.

The Autoharp Treasury series has been designed with clarity and convenience in mind. If you play your Autoharp on your lap or place it on a table, you can fold back the book to the desired page and insert it between the two rows of tuning pins on the slanted side of your instrument. The songs will then be in full view and both hands will be free for playing. I hope you and your friends and family will use this collection of songs to enrich your time together and utilize the Autoharp as the versatile, exciting instrument that it is.

Happy Strumming!
Meg Peterson
Maplewood, NJ
May, 2003

*Mel Bay Publications, Inc., Pacific, MO 63069: transposition, p. 164; simple strums, p. 18-32: melody picking, p.51-80; arpeggiando, p.23

Alphabetical Index of Song Titles

Hymns of Praise

All Hail the Power of Jesus' Name 9
A Mighty Fortress is Our God 14
Blest Be the Tie that Binds 8
Breathe on Me, Breath of God 11
Church's One Foundation, The 5
Come, Thou Almighty King 5
Doxology (Old Hundredth) 4
Fairest Lord Jesus 12
Faith of Our Fathers 16
Glorious Things of Thee are Spoken 6
Glory Be to the Father 16
God Be with You Till We Meet Again 12
God of Grace and God of Glory 5
God of Our Fathers 16
God the Omnipotent 11
In Christ There is No East or West 11
King of Love My Shepard Is, The 9
Love Divine, All Loves Excelling 10
My Faith Looks Up to Thee 10
Now All the Woods are Sleeping 9
Now the Day is Over 12
O Day of Rest and Gladness 8
O Jesus, I Have Promised 7
O Love, that Wilt Not Let Me Go 14
O Master, Let Me Walk with Thee 10
Once to Ev'ry Man and Nation 4
Onward, Christian Soldiers 13
Praise to the Lord, the Almighty 6
Rise Up, O Men of God! 4
Rock of Ages 6
Savior, Like a Shepard Lead Us 15
Shall We Gather at the River 15
Son of God Goes Forth to War, The 7
Spirit of God, Descend Upon My Heart 13
Sweet Hour of Prayer 8
Take My Life and Let It Be 7
This is My Father's World 15
We Would Be Building 9
What a Friend We Have in Jesus 14
When Morning Gilds the Skies 13
Where Cross the Crowded Way of Life 12
Ye Servants of God 11

Hymns Of Christmas

Angels, We Have Heard on High 19
As with Gladness Men of Old 20
Break Forth, O Beauteous Heavenly Light 21
First Noel, The 19
God Rest Ye Merry Gentlemen 19
Good Christian Men, Rejoice 23
Good King Wenceslas 18
Hark, the Herald Angels Sing 18
Holly and the Ivy, The 22
It Came Upon the Midnight Clear 18
Joy to the World 17
Lo, How a Rose E're Blooming 23
O Come, O Come, Emmanuel 17

Oh, Come All Ye Faithful 21
O Holy Night 22
O Little Town of Bethlehem (first version) 20
O Little Town of Bethlehem (second version) 20
Silent Night 17

Spirituals

All God's Chillun Got Wings 27
All Night, All Day 30
Deep River 32
Do, Lord 24
Down by the Riverside 35
Ev'ry Time I Feel the Spirit 30
Give Me that Old Time Religion 28
Good News 34
Go Down Moses 27
God Said to Noah 24
Gospel Train, The 27
Go Tell It on the Mountain 33
He's Got the Whole World in His Hands 34
Jacob's Ladder 29
Joshua Fought the Battle of Jerico 25
Lonesome Valley 25
Lord, I Want to Be a Christian 29
Mary Had a Baby 32
My Lord, What a Mornin' 28
Nobody Knows the Trouble I've Seen 26
One More River 33
Oh, Sinner Man 32
Poor Wayfaring Stranger 25
Rock-A My Soul 29
Sometimes I Feel Like a Motherless Child 31
Steal Away 26
Swing Low, Sweet Chariot 26
This Little Light of Mine 30
This Train 28
Train is A-Comin' 31
Wade in the Water 31
Were You There? 33

Hymns Of Thanksgiving

Bless Thou the Gifts 37
Break Thou the Bread of Life 36
Come, Ye Thankful People, Come 36
O God, Our Help in Ages Past 37
Thanksgiving Prayer (We Gather Together) 36
We Give Thee But Thine Own 37
We Plow the Fields 37

Hymns Of Easter and Lent

Abide with Me 38
Are Ye Able 38
Beneath the Cross of Jesus 39
Christ the Lord is Risen Today 38
Crown Him with Many Crowns 40
Hosanna, Loud Hosanna 39
Nearer My God to Thee 40

Hymns of Praise

Once to Ev'ry Man and Nation

Dm / A7 Dm Gm A7 Dm / F Gm A7 Dm Gm A7 Dm
Once to ev – 'ry man and na – tion, Comes the mo – ment to de – cide,

/ / A7 Dm Gm A7 Dm / F C A7 Dm Gm A7 Dm
In the strife of truth with false – hood, For the good or e – vil side;

F / C / Dm / A7 / B♭ / Gm / Dm Gm A7 /
Some great cause, God's new Mes – si – ah, Of – f'ring each the bloom or blight.

Dm / A7 Dm Gm A7 Dm / F Gm A7 Dm Gm A7 Dm
And the choice goes by for – ev – er, 'Twixt that dark – ness and that light.

2. By the light of burning martyrs, Jesus' bleeding feet I track,
Toiling up new Calv'ries ever, With the cross that turns not back;
New occasions teach new duties, Time makes ancient good uncouth,
They must upward still and onward, Who would keep abreast of truth.

Rise Up, O Men of God!

D7 G / / / C G C G D A7 D
Rise up, O men of God! Have done with les – ser things;

/ G D C G Am A7 D G C / / D7 G
Give heart and mind and soul and strength, To serve the King of kings.

2. Rise up, O men of God! His kingdom tarries long;
Bring in the day of brotherhood, And end the night of wrong.

Doxology

(Old Hundredth)
F Dm Am B♭ F Dm C F / / / C Dm B♭ F C
Praise God from whom all bless - ings flow; Praise Him, all crea – tures down be – low;

Dm C F C F B♭ C7 F C F Dm Gm / F C F
Praise Him a – bove ye heaven – ly host, Praise Fa - ther, Son and Ho – ly Ghost.

Come, Thou Almighty King

F   /   /   Gm F C7 F   /   C7 F B♭ / F C
Come, thou Al – migh – ty King, Help us Thy name to sing,

F   / / C   C7 F C7 F C7 F
Help us to praise! Fa – ther all glo – ri – ous,

C7 F C7 F C7 F /   / / / B♭ F B♭   F   C7 F
O'er all vic – to – ri – ous, Come and reign o – ver us, An – cient of days.

The Church's One Foundation

C / / F C   / G C F / G   G7 C
The Church's one Foun - da – tion, Is Je – sus Christ her Lord;

G7 C / E7 / / F   G F   G7 C D7 G
She is His new cre – a – tion, By wa – ter and the word;

G7 C   G7 C F /   C Am / E7 Am A7 Dm
From heaven He came and sought her, To be His ho - ly Bride:

G7 C / F   C F   Dm F / Dm F G7 C
With His own blood He bought her, And for her life He died.

2. Elect from every nation, Yet one o'er all the earth,
Her charter of salvation, One Lord, one faith, one birth;
One holy name she blesses, Partakes one holy food,
And to one hope she presses, With every grace endued.

God of Grace and God of Glory

F B♭ F /   / / /   C7 F / B♭ Gm F C7 F
God of grace and God of glo – ry, On Thy peo – ple pour Thy power;

/   B♭ F /   / / /   C7 F B♭ F B♭ F   C7 F
Crown Thine An – cient church's sto – ry, Bring her bud to glor – ious flower.

C7 F C7 / F C7 F / / / C7   F C7 F C7
Grant us wis – dom, grant us cour – age, For the fac – ing of this hour.

F C7 F B♭ F C7 F
For the fac – ing of this hour.

Praise to the Lord, the Almighty

```
F    Dm C  F    C  F  Am    B♭ F  B♭  C7 Dm  Gm C7   F
```
Praise to   the Lord, the Al – might – ty, The King of cre – a   –   tion!

```
/ Dm  C    F    C    F  Am B♭ F  B♭   C7 Dm   Gm C7   F
```
O my soul, praise Him, For He is thy health and sal – va   –   tion!

```
/  /  /   B♭   F    C7 F  C    C7 F    C    F  B♭  A7 Dm  C    F  Gm C7    F
```
All ye who hear, Now to His tem – ple draw near; Join me in glad ad – o – ra   –   tion.

2. Praise to the Lord, who o'er all things, So wondrously reigneth,
Shieldeth thee under His wings, Yea, so gently sustaineth!
Hast thou not seen how thy desires e'er have been, Granted in what He ordaineth?

Rock of Ages

```
G   C G / C   /  G   / D7 G  Am  G  D7  G
```
Rock of ages, cleft for me, Let me hide my – self in   Thee,

```
D7 G D7 /  /  /   G     D7 G  D7    /  /   /    G
```
Let the wa – ter and the blood, From Thy wound – ed side which flowed

```
 / C G /  C    /  G    /  D7 G   Am G   D7 G
```
Be of sin the dou – ble cure, Save from wrath and make me pure.

Glorious Things of Thee are Spoken

```
C   G7  C   G  G7 C  G7  C   F   C  G7 C  D7 /  G
```
Glo – rious things of Thee are spo – ken, Zi – on, ci – ty of our God,

```
C  G7   C   G   G7 C  G7 C   F     C  G7 C  D7 /  G
```
He whose word can – not be bro – ken, Formed thee for His own a – bode;

```
 /  C  G   / G7 C  G     /  C   G7 Am /   D7 /    G    G7
```
On the Rock of A – ges found – ed, What can shake thy sure re – pose?

```
 C  /    F  C   F  / C   G7   C  G   G7   C   F C G7 C
```
With sal – va – tion's walls   sur – round – ed, Thou mayest smile at all thy foes.

2. See the streams of living waters, Springing from eternal love,
Well supply thy sons and daughters, And all fear of want remove;
Who can faint while such a river Ever flows their thirst to assuage?
Grace which, like the Lord, the Giver, Never fails from age to age.

Take My Life and Let It Be

F   C7 F   / C7 F C F   Bb   / F Dm G7 C
Take my life, and let it be, Con – se – cra – ted, Lord, to Thee,

F   C7 F   /   C7 F C   F Bb F / C7   F   /
Take my mo – ments and my days; Let them flow in ceas – less praise.

C7 Bb C7   /   F C7 F   C7 F C7 Gm F C7 F
Take my hands and let them move, At the im – pulse of Thy love.

  / C7 F   / C7 F   C7 F   Bb F   / C7 F /
Take my feet and let them be, Swift and beau – ti – ful for Thee.

O Jesus, I Have Promised

   F /   /   /   / /   C   /   C7 /   / /   F   //
O Je – sus, I have prom – ised, To serve   Thee to the end;

  / D7 /   /   / / Gm   / G7 /   /   /   C   /   C7
Be Thou for – ev – er near me, My Mas – ter and my Friend;

/ F   /   / /   / // C7 //   /   /   / F //
I shall not fear the bat – tle, If Thou art by my side,

  / D7 /   /   /   / // Gm / Bb /   / C7 F   //
Nor wan – der from the path – way, If Thou wilt be my Guide.

2. O let me feel Thee near me! The world is ever near;
I see the sights that dazzle, The tempting sounds I hear.
My foes are ever near me, Around me and within;
But, Jesus, draw Thou nearer, And shield my soul from sin.

The Son of God Goes Forth to War

Bb / F7 Bb   / Eb F7 /   Bb F   Bb F7 Bb F
The Son of God goes forth to war, A   king – ly crown to gain;

/ Bb   F7   Bb D7 /   Eb   /   /   Bb   / F7 Bb /
His blood – stained ban – ner streams a – far; Who fol – lows in   His train?

  / Gm / D7   / Gm / Eb   /   Bb   / F7 /   Bb
Who best can drink His cup of woe, Tri – umph – ant o – ver pain,

F7 Bb F7 Bb   / Eb F7   /   Bb Gm Eb   / F7 Bb
Who pa – tient bears His cross be – low; He   fol – lows in His train.

O Day of Rest and Gladness

```
    D    A7    D    /    /    A7    D    /
```
O day of rest and gladness,   O day of joy and light;

```
    /        A7    D    /    /    A7    D    /
```
A balm for care and sadness,   Most beauti – ful and bright!

```
    G        /    D    /        /    A7    D    /
```
This day the meek and lowly,   Bowed down be – fore the throne,

```
    G7    /    D    /    /    A7    D    /
```
Sing, holy, holy, holy,   Is the E – ternal One.

2. This day, on hungry nations, The heav'nly manna falls,
To holy convocations, The gospel message calls;
The light from heav'n is glowing, And living waters flowing, In soul refreshing streams.

Sweet Hour of Prayer

```
    C    /        F    /    C    /    G7        /
```
Sweet hour of prayer, sweet hour of prayer; That calls me from a world of care,

```
    C    /    F        /    C    /    G7    C
```
And bids me at my Fa – ther's throne, Make all my wants and wishes known.

```
    /    F    C    /    /    F    C    G
```
In seasons of dis – tress and grief, My soul has often found re – lief,

```
    C    /        F    /    C    /    G7    C
```
And oft es – caped the tempter's snare, By thy re – turn, sweet hour of prayer.

2. Sweet hour of prayer, sweet hour of prayer; Thy wings shall my petition bear
To Him whose truth and faithfulness, Engage the waiting soul to bless;
And since He bids me seek His face, Believe His word and trust His grace,
I'll cast on Him my ev'ry care, And wait for thee, sweet hour of prayer.

Blest Be the Tie that Binds

```
G  /  / D7 /  G  /  /  C  / G    / D7  /
```
Blest be the tie that binds   Our hearts in Christ – ian love;

```
/  /  /  G  / D7  / G   C G C G D7 G  /
```
The fel – low – ship of kind – dred minds, Is like to that a – bove.

All Hail the Power of Jesus' Name

```
  C  F   /   /    / C  Dm  C     F  C  Dm F    C    F
All hail the pow'r of Je – sus' name, Let an - gels pros - trate fall;

  C    F   C  F   / F C7 F   C    F     C   Dm  C  G7  C
Bring forth the roy - al  di - a - dem, And crown Him Lord  of       all.

  F    /   /   /    / C  /   /    Dm  F   B♭  F   C7    F
Bring forth the roy - al  di - a - dem, And crown Him Lord     of  all.
```

We Would Be Building

(tune: Finlandia)
```
F  C    F  C7   F  C   F B♭  C  / F /  C    F   C7  F  C   F B♭   C F
We would be build - ing; tem - ples still un - done, O'er crum - bling walls their cross - es scarce - ly lift;

  /   /   / Dm  /  /  Am /  C   /  Gm  /  F   C  F  /  B♭   Gm /  A7  /
Wait - ing till love can raise the bro - ken stone,     And hearts cre - a - tive bridge  the  hu - man rift.

  F   /   / Dm  /   /    F  C  /  /  Gm  /  F   C F  /  B♭  Gm  C7  F  /
We would be build - ing; Mas - ter, let Thy plan      Re - veal the life that God would give to man.
```

Now All the Woods are Sleeping

```
  F  B♭  C   F    / B♭  C7 F  /   /   / C    Am Dm  G7  C
Now all  the woods are sleep –  ing, And night and still – ness creep –  ing

C7 Dm  C  F   B♭  C   A   Dm  C  F  D7 Gm  D
O'er ci –  ty, man, and beast, But thou, my heart,  a – wake thee

Dm  F    /  C   A7  Dm G7  C    C7 Dm  C  F   Gm  F  C7  F
To  prayer a – while  be – take      thee, And praise thy ma – ker 'ere thou rest.
```

The King of Love My Shepherd Is

```
F  C   B♭ C7 F  /  C7   A7 Dm  C7    F   /   G7   / F  / C
The King  of  love my shep – herd is,  Whose good – ness fail – eth nev – er;

F  B♭   C7 F  Dm Gm  A7  Dm  B♭  C7  B♭  C7  F   C7  F
I  noth – ing lack if  I   am  His, And He  is  mine for – ev – er.
```

My Faith Looks Up to Thee

```
 C  /   /   G  G7 C    G7    /   /  /   C   G7
```
My faith looks up to Thee, Thou, Lamb of Cal – va – ry,

```
C   G  D7  G  G7 C    /  G7  C   F  C    /   /  G7  C  F   C
```
Sav – ior di – vine: Now hear me while I   pray,   Take all my guilt a – way,

```
 / G  F  C   G7  C  / Dm   G7   C
```
O let me from this day be whol – ly   Thine!

2. May Thy rich grace impart strength to my fainting heart,
My zeal inspire: As Thou hast died for me,
O may my love to Thee
Pure, warm and changeless be, a living fire!

O Master, Let Me Walk with Thee

```
C  /   /  F  C  Dm  D7  G  /  /   G7  C   Am  D7   /   G
```
O Mas – ter, let me walk with Thee In low – ly paths of   ser – vice free;

```
G7  F  G7  C   Em  F  C  G7   C  G7  Am  G7  C  Dm  / G7  C
```
Tell me Thy sec - ret, help me bear, The strain of toil, the fret   of care.

2. Help me the slow of heart to move, By some clear winning word of love;
Teach me the wayward feet to stay, And guide them in the homeward way.

Love Divine, All Loves Excelling

```
B♭  /   E♭  B♭  /  F7   /   B♭  E♭  /  /   /   B♭   F7   B♭
```
Love di – vine, all love ex – cell – ing, Joy of Heav'n to earth come down!

```
 /  / E♭  B♭  /   F7  D7  Gm  E♭  /   B♭   /  F7   /   B♭
```
Fix in us Thy hum – ble dwell – ing;   All Thy faith – ful mer – cies crown.

```
Gm  /   /  D7 Gm  /   D   /   B♭   /   E♭    B♭  F  C7  F  F7
```
Je – sus, Thou art all com – pas – sion, Pure; un – bound – ed love Thou art;

```
B♭  /   E♭  B♭  /  F7  D7  Gm  E♭  /  B♭  / F7    /   B♭
```
Vis – it us with Thy sal – va – tion; En – ter ev' – ry trem – bling heart.

2. Breathe, O breathe Thy loving Spirit Into every troubled breast!
Let us all in Thee inherit, Let us find that second rest,
Take away our bent to sinning. Alpha and Omega be;
End of faith, as its beginning, Set our hearts at liberty.

Breathe on Me, Breath of God

F   / /   **Bb**   /   **F**   /   **C7 F Gm G7 C**
Breathe on me, Breath of God, Fill me with life   a – new,

F   **Bb**   /   **F**   /   /   **Gm**   /   /   **F C7 F**   /   **C7**   **F**
That I may love what Thou dost love, And do   what Thou wouldst do.

2. Breathe on me, Breath of God, Until me heart is pure,
Until with Thee I will one will, To do and to endure.

God the Omnipotent!

C F   /   **C**   /   /   **Am G F**   **C**   **A7 Dm**   **G7**   /   **C**   /**Am B7 Em**   **B7**   /   **Em**
God the om – ni – po – tent! King, who or – dain – est, Thun – der Thy clar – ion,   the light – ning Thy sword;

G7   **C G C**   / **E7 Am**   /   **E7 F**   **G7 Am G F C**   /**Dm C G7 C**
Show forth Thy pit – y   on   high where Thou reign – est, Give to us peace in our time, O Lord.

2. God the all merciful! Earth hath forsaken, Thy ways all holy and slighted Thy word;
Let not Thy wrath in its terrors awaken. Give to us peace in our time, O Lord.

Ye Servants of God

C7 F   /   **C F**   /   **Bb**   **Gm C7**   **F**   **C F**   **C G7 C**   **F C**   **F G7 C**
Ye serv – ants of God, your Mas – ter pro – claim, And pu – blish a – broad His won – der – ful Name;

A7 Dm Gm A7 Dm   /   **C7 F**   **C G7 C**   /   **Bb**   **C7 F C**   /   **F Gm**   /   **C7 F**
The Name all vic – to – rious of Je – sus ex – tol; His King – dom is glo – rious and rules o – ver all.

2. God ruleth on high, almighty to save; And still He is nigh, His presence we have.
The great congregation His triumph shall sing, Ascribing salvation to Jesus, our King.

In Christ There is No East or West

G7   **C**   **Em F C G7**   /   **C**   /**G C G7**   **C G**
In   Christ there is no East or West, In Him no South or North;

C F C   **F C**   **G G7 Am**   /   **C Dm C**   **G7**   **C**
But one great fellow – ship of love, Through – out the whole wide earth.

2. In Him shall true hearts ev'ry where, Their high communion find;
His service is the golden chord, Close binding all mankind.

Where Cross the Crowded Ways of Life

```
  F    /   C7  F     Gm  C7  A7  Dm  G7    C     G7  C   / F  C  G7  C
```
Where cross the crowd – ed ways of life, Where sound the cries of race   and clan,

```
C7  F   /   C7  /   F    /  B♭   B♭  C7   /  Dm  Gm  F  Gm  C7  F
```
A – bove the noise of self – ish strife, We hear Thy voice, O Son   of man!

2. In haunts of wretchedness and need, On shadowed thresholds dark with fears,
From paths where hide the lures of greed, We catch the visions of Thy tears.

Fairest Lord Jesus

```
 C   Am  /   Dm G7  C   /   / Am  /   Dm  G  C   /  F    / C    G7 C  F G7  C  G   /
```
Fair – est Lord Je   –   sus, Rul – er of all na   –   ture, O Thou of God   and   man   the Son;

```
 C   F   C A7  / Dm  /   A7  Dm  /  G7  C   /   E7  Am   C7  F   C  G7   C
```
Thee will I cher – ish, Thee will I hon – or, Thou, my soul's glo – ry, joy, and crown.

Now the Day is Over

```
C    / G7 / C / / /  Am   / E7    / Am / / / D7  /     / / G  /   / / G7  /   /  /  C  //
```
Now the day is o – ver, Night is draw – ing nigh;   Shad – ows of the eve – ning Steal   a – cross the sky.

2. Jesus give the weary Calm and sweet repose; With Thy tenderest blessing May our eyelids close.
3. When the morning wakens, Then may I arise; Pure and fresh and sinless, In Thy holy eyes.

God Be with You Till We Meet Again

```
 C /   /     /     /  G  C  F/   /     /     / /     C
```
God   be with you till we meet a - gain; By   His counsels guide, uphold   you,

```
 G /    /      /     C / /  / /     F  C  /  G7  C  G7  C
```
With   His sheep se - cure - ly fold you; God   be with you till we meet a - gain.

```
      C // /     F // /     C /  /  /  G //
```
Till we meet,   till we meet,   Till we meet at Je - sus feet;

```
      C // /      F // C /    F  C  / G7  C  G7  C
```
Till we meet,   till we meet,   God   be with you till we meet a- gain.

2. God be with you till we meet again; 'Neath His wings protecting, hide you,
Daily manna still provide you; God be with you till we meet again.

When Morning Gilds the Skies

C   G7   C   F   / G7 F G7 Am E7 Am   /   D7
When Morn – ing gilds the skies,   My heart a – wak – ing, cries,

/ G   Am D7 G   /   /   C   / G7 C   G7
May Je – sus Christ be praised! A – like at work and prayer,

/ C   Am D7 /   G   G7 C   C7   F   G   C
To Je – sus   I   re – pair; May Je – sus Christ be praised!

2. Whene'er the sweet church bell, Peals over hill and dell,
May Jesus Christ be praised! O hark to what it sings,
As joyously it rings, May Jesus Christ be praised!

Spirit of God, Descend Upon My Heart

B♭   / /   F7 B♭ E♭ B♭ E♭ F7 B♭   Gm A7 /   Dm   G7   F / Gm   C7   F
Spi – rit of God, des – cend up – on my heart; Wean it from earth, through all its puls – es move.

/   / / F7   E♭ F7   E♭ F7 E7 F7 B♭ F   B♭ F   E♭ B♭ E♭ B♭   F7 B♭
Stoop to my weak – ness, might – y   as Thou art, And make me love Thee as I   ought to love.

2. Hast Thou not bid us love Thee, God and King? All, all Thine own, soul, heart and strength and mind;
I see Thy cross, there teach my heart to cling: O let me seek Thee and O let me find.

Onward, Christian Soldiers

C   /   /   / G / / /   G7   / F G7 C ///
On – ward, Chris – tian sol – diers! March – ing as to war,

/   /   /   / // G / Am /   / D7 G   ///
With the cross of Je – sus Go-ing on be - fore,

/   / /   / C / // / / /   / F ///
Christ, the roy – al Mas – ter, Leads a – gainst the foe;

/   C   F   C F C F C F   C   F   C   G ///
For – ward in – to bat – tle   See His ban - ners go!

C   /   /   / / G / / G7   / / / C ///
On – ward, Chris – tian sol – diers! March – ing as to war,

/   /   / G7 C / // F   C G7 /   C   //
With the cross of Je – sus Go - ing on   be – fore.

13

O Love, that Wilt Not Let Me Go

```
   F        /              / C7   C7      /         /        /
O Love that wilt not let me go,      I rest my weary soul in Thee;

   F       A7         / Dm     G7      /           F       /    / C7    F
I give Thee back the life I owe,      That in Thy ocean depths its flow may richer, full – er  be.
```

2. O Light that follow'st all my way, I yield my flick'ring torch to Thee;
My heart restores its borrowed ray, That in Thy sunshine blaze its day may brighter, fairer be.

A Mighty Fortress is Our God

```
C  /     / G    / Am D7 G   Am Em   F    C  A7 Dm G7  C
A might – y fort – ress is  our God, A    bul – wark nev – er fail    – ing

   /   /    / G  / Am D7  G   Am Em   F  C  A7  Dm G7  C
Our Help – er He, a – mid the  flood, Of  mor – tal ills pre – vail    – ing;

   /   / Am  G   D7  G   Am  G   C   F   E7  Am
For still our  an – cient foe, Doth seek to work his  woe;

 E7 Am  G  Am        D7  G    F    /    C  A7  Dm  E7
His craft and pow – er are great, And armed with cru – el    hate.

Am  Em  F  C  A7  Dm G7  C
On  earth is not his  e – qual.
```

What a Friend We Have in Jesus

```
F   / /       /     Bb / / / F / /        /        C   ///
What a friend we have in Je – sus,   All our sins and griefs to bear!

F    /   /    /    Bb / / / F  /       /       C7    F  / //
What a privi – lege to car – ry    Ev – 'ry – thing to God in prayer!

C7 /      /        /     F  / / / Bb /   F         /        C  ///
Oh,  what peace we oft – ten for – feit,   Oh, what need – less pain we bear,

F /      /        /    Bb / / / F /     /       C7    F    / /
All be – cause we do not car – ry,    Ev – 'ry – thing to God in prayer.
```

2. Have we trials and temptations? Is there trouble anywhere?
We should never be discouraged; Take it to the Lord in prayer.
Can we find a friend so faith – ful, Who will all our sorrows share?
Jesus knows our every weakness; Take it to the Lord in prayer.

This is My Father's World

```
 C  /  /  /   G7   C    / C7   /  F  / C     /   G      //
This is my Fa – ther's world,         And to my lis – t'ning ears
```

```
G7  C    /   /   /   E7   /  Am  G7  C   / G7 /    C       //
All  na – ture sings and round me rings, The mus-ic of   the spheres.
```

```
 G7  C /  F   G7    C    // /  F   / G F  C       //
This is my Fa – ther's world:      I  rest me in the thought
```

```
G7   C    /   /   /   E7   /  Am  G7  C    / G7     /   C        //
Of  rocks and trees, of  skies and seas; His hand the won – ders wrought.
```

2. This is my Father's world, The birds their carols raise,
The morning light, the lily white, Declare their maker's praise.
This is my Father's world, He shines in all that's fair;
In the rushing grass I hear Him pass, He speaks to me ev'rywhere.

Savior, Like a Shepherd Lead Us

```
C    /  /    /       / / //  G7   C   G7      /    C  ///
Sav - ior, like a shepherd lead us, Much we need Thy tender care;
```

```
 /  /  /     /      / / //  G7  C  G7      /        C //
In Thy pleasant pastures feed  us, For our use Thy folds pre - pare;
```

```
 /    F  // /     C   // /       G7   /  /   / C //
Blessed Je - sus, Blessed Je - sus, Thou hast bought us, Thine we are;
```

```
 /    F  // /     C   // /       /    / G7  / C //
Blessed Je - sus, Blessed Je - sus, Thou hast bought us, Thine we are.
```

Shall We Gather at the River

```
 C   /  /    / /  //  //  G7   /    /   /  /   //  //
Shall we gather at the  riv - er, Where bright angel feet have trod;
```

```
 C   /  /    /      // /  /    G7 /  /   /  C ///
With its crystal tide for - ev - er, Flowing by the throne of God?
```

```
 F   /  /   /    C/ //  G7   /     /    / C / //
Yes, we'll gather at the riv - er, The beauti - ful, the beauti - ful  riv - er,
```

```
 F    /    /  /   C // /  G7  /    /    / C //
Gather with the saints at the riv - er  That flows by the throne of God.
```

Glory Be to the Father

```
F  /  /  /     C  /  //
```
Glo – ry be to the Fa – ther,

```
 / / / F  C   G7 C F C /  G7 /  C    //
```
And to the Son, and to the Ho – ly   Ghost;

```
C7 F  /  /  /  /     /   C7 /
```
As it was in the be - gin – ing,

```
 /  /  /     /  /  /  /  F  //
```
Is now   and ev-er shall be,

```
 /   /  /       /  Bb /  Gm /  C7 /  /  /  F
```
World   with – out end,   A – men, A – men.

Faith of Our Fathers

```
F            /        Gm  C7 F  Bb        F        G7      C
```
Faith of our Fa – thers liv – ing still, In spite of dun – geon, fire, and sword;

```
F            /        Gm  C7 F  Bb            F        G7 C7   F
```
Oh, how our hearts beat high with joy, When - e'er we hear that glo - rious word!

```
Bb          F     C  F  /        Bb   C7     F  Bb F
```
Faith of our fathers! Holy faith! We will be true to thee till death! A – men.

God of Our Fathers

```
 C  Am G  C  F   C  /  /  G7 C
```
God of our fa - thers, whose al - might - y hand

```
 /    Am /  Em A7 G  /  /  D7 G
```
Leads forth in beau - ty   all thy star - ry band

```
 /  /  /  Eb  /  Gm  /  /  D7 G  G7
```
Of shin - ing worlds in splen - dor through the skies,

```
 C  G    F  C  A7 Dm  C  Dm G7 C
```
Our grate - ful songs be - fore Thy throne a - rise.

Hymns of Christmas

Joy to the World

```
C  F      C   F    C  G7  C   /
```
Joy to the world, the Lord is come!

```
   F   /    G7 /      C  / / /
```
Let earth re - ceive   her King!

```
  C   F  C/       /   F   C   /
```
Let ev - 'ry heart pre - pare Him room,

```
  /        /     / /     G7        /    / /
```
And heav'n and nature sing, And heav'n and nature sing,

```
  C    F     C  /    C  G7   C
```
And heav'n,   and heav'n and na - ture sing.

Silent Night

```
C F C   /    / F C /    G7 / /   C  / /  C7 F     /   / G7 F C    F C   /
```
Si - lent night, ho - ly night, all is calm, all is bright.   Round yon Vir - gin Moth - er and Child,

```
F   / /  G7 F C  F  C  /   G7 / /   /   / C /   /   / / G7   /   / C
```
Ho - ly In - fant so ten - der and mild, Sleep in heav - en - ly peace. Sle - ep in heav - en - ly peace.

O Come, O Come, Emmanuel

```
  Dm      F       Gm C7   Dm  C   F      Bb   Gm /  Dm
```
O come, O come, Em - ma - nu - el,   And ran - som cap - tive Is - ra - el,

```
   Gm       /     Dm G7   C  Dm C    F    Gm  C7  F
```
That mourns in lone - ly ex - ile here, Un - til the Son of God   ap - pear.

```
/   C   Dm  Am   F  Gm C7  Dm  C   F    Bb    Gm /    Dm
```
Re - joice! Re - joice! Em-man - u - el shall come to thee, O Is - ra - el.

2. O come Thou Rod of Jesse, Free Thine own from Satan's tyranny;
From depths of hell Thy people save, And give them vict'ry o'er the grave.
Rejoice! Rejoice! Emmanuel shall come to thee, O Israel.

17

Hark, the Herald Angels Sing

| F | / | / C7 | Dm F | /C | F | / B♭ / | F | C7 F |

Hark, the her -' ald an - gels sing, "Glo - ry to   the new - born King;

| / | / | / C7 | Dm | F G7 /C | / | / / | / | G7 C |

Peace on earth   and mer - cy mild, God and sin - ners re - con - ciled."

| F | / | / | / C7 | F | /C | F | / / | / | B♭ F | /C |

Joy - ful all ye na - tions rise, Join the tri - umph of the skies;

| B♭ | / | / | D7 Gm D7 | Gm | / | C | C7 F | / | Dm C | F | / |

With th'an - gel - ic host pro - claim, "Christ is born in Beth - le - hem."

| B♭ | / | / | D7 Gm D7 | Gm | / | C C7 F | / | B♭ C7 | F |

Hark the her - ald   an - gels   sing, "Glo - ry to   the new - born King!"

It Came Upon the Midnight Clear

| F | B♭ | F | / | B♭ | G7 | C C7 |

It came up - on the midnight clear, That glorious song of old,

| F | B♭ | F | / | B♭ | C7 | F / |

From an - gels bending near the earth To touch their harps of gold.

| A7 | / | Dm | / | C | G7 | C C7 |

"Peace on the earth, good will to men, From Heav'n's all gracious King!"

| F | B♭ | F | / | B♭ | C7 | F / |

The world in solemn stillness lay, To hear the angels sing.

Good King Wenceslas

| F | / | Dm C | F | / | C B♭ F | B♭ C7 B♭ | F |

Good King Wen - ces - las look'd out, On the Feast of Ste - phen,

| / | / Dm C | F | / | C B♭ | F | B♭ C7 B♭ | F |

When the snow lay round a - bout, Deep, and crisp, and e - ven;

| / | C7 F | C7 F | C7 Dm | B♭ | F B♭ C7 B♭ | F |

Bright - ly shone the moon that night, Though the frost was cru - el;

| / | / B♭ C7 Dm G7 | C | F | B♭ F C7 Dm B♭ | F |

When a poor man came in sight, Gath' - ring win - ter fu - el.

Angels We Have Heard on High

F / Am / C7 / F //   C7 F   / / C7   F /
An - gels we have heard on high, Sweet - ly   sing - ing o'er the plains,

/   /   Am   /   C7 /   F / / C7 /   /   F   C7   F   /
And the moun - tains in   re - ply,   E - cho - ing their joy   -   ous strains:

Refrain:
F   / D7 / Gm / C7 / F / Bb / C G7   C C7 F C7 F Bb   F / C7 /
Glo- - - - - - - - - - - - - - - - - ri - a,   In ex - cel - sis De - o,

F   / D7 / Gm / C7 / F / Bb / C G7   C C7 F C7 F Bb   F / C7 / F
Glo- - - - - - - -- - - - - - - - ri - a,   In ex - cel - sis De - - - - o.

2. Shepherds why this jubilee? Why your joyous strains prolong?
What the gladsome tiding be, Which inspire your heavenly song? *Refrain*

God Rest Ye Merry Gentlemen

   Dm   A7   Dm   /   Bb   /   A7 /
God rest you merry gentle - men let nothing you dis - may,

   Dm   A7   Dm   /   Bb   /   A7   D7
Re - member, Christ our sav - ior was born on Christmas day

   Gm   C7   F   A7   Dm   /   C
To save us all from Satan's power when we were gone a-stray

C7   F   /   A7   /   Bb   Dm   C
 O   ti - dings of com - fort and joy,   comfort and joy,

C7   F   /   A7   /   Dm
 O   ti - dings of com - fort and joy.

The First Noel

G7   C   Am G F G7 C G   F C   F G7 C G   F   C   F   G7 C   / G7   C
The first No - el the   an - gels did say, Was to cer - tain poor shep - herds in fields as they lay.

G7 C   Am   G   F G7 C   G F   C   F G7 C G   F   C F G7 C / G7 C
In fields where they lay   keep - ing their sheep, On a cold win - ter's night that was so deep.

G7   C Am G C   F /   C Am G F C F G7 C / G7 C
No - el. No - el. No - el. No - el. Born is the King of Is - ra - el.

O Little Town of Bethlehem (first version)

```
    F    /    Gm    /        F    C7    F  /
O lit - tle town of Beth - le - hem, How still we see thee lie;

     /    D7    Gm    /    F    C7    F  /
A - bove thy deep and dream - less sleep, The si - lent stars go by.

     /    Gm    A7  /    Dm    /    A7  /
Yet,  in thy dark streets shin - eth, The  ev - er - last - ing light,

     F    /    Gm    /    F    C7    F  /
The hopes and fears of all the years, Are met in thee to - night.
```

O Little Town of Bethlehem (second version)

```
C7 F Bb F C7 F Dm Am  F  Bb F Gm C7  F
 O lit - tle town of Beth - le - hem, How still we  see  thee lie;

C7   F  Bb F  C7  F     Dm Am  F  Bb  F  Gm C7  F
 A - bove thy deep and dream - less  sleep, The  si - lent stars   go by.

Dm Am /   C7   /    Dm / C  C7   F  /   Bb  /  C7  /  Bb
Yet,  in    thy dark streets shin - eth, The  ev - er - last - ing light,

 C7   F    Bb   F  C7  F Dm Am   F  Bb  F   Gm C7    F
The hopes and fears of  all  the  years, Are met in  thee  to - night.
```

As with Gladness Men of Old

```
F  C7 F C7   F    Bb  C7  F  Bb  C7  F   Bb   F  C7  F
As with    glad - ness  men of  old, Did  the  guid - ing  star be - hold;

F  C7 F C7   F    Bb    C7  F   Bb  C7 F   Bb    F   C7  F
As with    joy  they  hailed its  light, Lead - ing on - ward,  beam - ing  bright;

/   C   Dm  /    C   C7     F  Bb C7 Dm Gm F  C7  F
So,  most gra - cious Lord,   may we, Ev - er - more be led  to Thee.
```

2. As with joyful steps they sped, To that lowly manger bed,
There to bend the knee before, Him whom heav'n and earth adore,
So may we with willing feet, Ever seek Thy mercy seat.

Oh, Come, All Ye Faithful (Adeste Fideles)

```
F   //  / / C7/  //  F  C7 F  Bb  F / C7
```
Oh, come, all ye faith - ful, Joy - ful and tri - um - phant,

```
Dm  / G7 C  G7  C G7 C  F  C / G7 /    C / C7 /
```
Oh, come ye, Oh, come ye to Beth - le - hem.

```
 F /  C7 F  Bb C7 F /  C  A7  Dm  G7 C / G7 C
```
Come and be - hold Him Born the King of an - gels

```
F  /   C F C7 F / /   / /   C  F Bb F / C
```
Oh, come, let us a- dore Him, Oh, come, let us a - dore Him,

```
F  Bb  F C  Dm C7 /  Dm Gm  F / C7 /   F //
```
Oh, come, let us a - dore Him,   Christ   the Lord.

2. Sing, choirs of angels, sing in exultation,
Oh, sing, all ye citizens of heaven above.
Glory to God, all glory in the highest;
Oh, come, let us adore Him, Oh, come, let us adore Him,
Oh, come, let us adore Him, Christ, the Lord!

Break Forth, O Beauteous Heavenly Light

```
 F  Dm C F    C  Dm  G7  C  A7 Bb C F C F C C7 F
```
Break forth, O beau - teous heav'n - ly light, And ush - er in the morn - ing!

```
 / Dm   C    F   C Dm G7  C  A7 Bb C F C   F   C C7 F
```
Ye shep - herds, shrink not with af - fright, But hear the an - gels' warn - ing.

```
 C  /   D7 Gm / D7 / Gm  F D7 /  Gm  / /   A7 Dm
```
This child, now weak in in - fan - cy, Our con - fi - dence and joy shall be,

```
 C  F    / Bb C F G7 / C  F  Bb  F Bb C F Gm C7 F
```
The pow'r of Sa - tan break - ing, Our peace e - ter - nal mak - ing.

2. All blessing, thanks and praise to Thee, Lord Jesus Christ, be given:
Thou hast our brother deigned to be, Our foes in sunder riven.
O grant us through our day of grace, With constant praise to seek Thy face;
Grant us ere long in glory, With praises to adore Thee.

The Holly and the Ivy

```
     F   /  Bb  F  /  /  /   Dm      /  Bb  C   /
```
The holly and the i - vy,   When they are both full grown,

```
 /   F    /  /    Bb    C   Dm  F   /   C7   F
```
Of all the trees that are in the wood, The holly bears the crown.

Refrain:
```
     F   / Bb  F  /  /      Dm     /  Bb  C
```
The rising of the sun,   And the running of the deer,

```
 /    F    /  /   Bb    F    Dm   F    /  C7  F
```
The playing of the merry organ, Sweet singing of the choir.

2. The holly bears a blossom, As white as the lily flow'r.
And Mary bore sweet Jesus Christ, To be our sweet Savoir. *Refrain*

O Holy Night

```
Bb  /   /  /     Eb     /    Bb  /  /
```
 O ho - ly night, the stars are brightly shin - ing,

```
  /   /   /   F7   /    Bb  /  /  /
```
It is the night of the dear Savior's birth;

```
  /   /     /  /   Eb    /   Bb  /  /
```
Long lay the world   in sin and error pin - ing

```
  Bb    Dm   /     A7   /    Dm  /  /  /
```
Till He ap - peared and the soul felt its worth.

```
  F7  /  /   /  Bb       /       /    /
```
A thrill of hope the wear - ry world re - joic - es,

```
  F7  /  /   /  Bb     /         /  /
```
For yon - der breaks a new and glo - rious morn!

```
Gm / / /      Dm  / / /  Cm  / /   /   Gm  / / /
```
 Fall   on your knees!   O hear   the an - gel voi - ces,

```
  Bb  / F7 /    Bb  / Eb / Bb / F7       /      Bb  / /
```
O night   di - vine!   O night   when Christ was born!

```
 / F7 / / /      Bb / Eb  /  Bb  / F7          Bb  / /
```
O night   di - vine! O night,   O night di - vine!

22

Good Christian Men, Rejoice

      F   /   C   /   F   /   C   /
Good Christian men, re - joice,   With heart and soul and voice;

F   C   F   Dm Gm C7   F   /
Give ye heed to what we say; Jesus Christ is born to - day:

/   C   F   Dm   Gm C7 Dm   /
Ox and ass be - fore Him bow, And He is in the man - ger now.

 Bb   C   Dm C F   C7   F /
Christ is born to - day!   Christ is born to - day!

2. Good Christian men, rejoice, With heart and soul and voice;
Now ye hear of endless bliss; Jesus Christ was born for this!
He hath oped the heav'nly door, And man is bless-ed evermore.
Christ was born for this! Christ was born for this!

Lo, How a Rose E'er Blooming

F / / Bb F C   Dm Bb F   C Dm   Bb C7   F
Lo, how a Rose e'er bloom - ing, From ten - der   stem   hath sprung!

 / / / Bb F   C Dm Bb F C Dm C7   F
Of Je - se's lin - eage com - ing, As men of   old   have sung.

/ C   / F   G7 C   /   / F Bb F C   D7
It came, a flow - 'ret bright, A - mid the cold of win - ter,

Gm F C Dm   Bb C7 F
When half spent   was   the   night.

2. Isaiah 'twas foretold it, The Rose I have in mind,
With Mary we behold it, The Virgin Mother kind.
To show God's love aright, She bore to men a Savior,
When half spent was the night.

Spirituals

God Said to Noah

```
C    /  /  /        F   /  G7  /   C    /  /  /         F   /  G7   /
```
God said to Noah, there's gonna be a floody floody, God said   to Noah, there's gonna be   a floody, floody,

```
C   /   C7  /  F   /     C    /    /   / G7  / C //
```
Get those child - ren ⁊ out of the muddy, muddy, Children   of the Lord.

Chorus:
```
G7 C /   /  /       F     /    G7    /    C /    /  /      F      /     G7    /
```
So rise and shine and give God the glory, glory, Rise and shine   and give God   the glory, glory,

```
C   /  C7  /  F      /       C    /    /   / G7  / C //
```
Rise and shine and ⁊ give God the glory, glory, Children   of the Lord.

Do, Lord

```
F       /       /     /      /       /     / F7
```
I've got a home in glory - land that out - shines   the sun.

```
B♭      /       /     /      /       /   F /
```
I've got a home in glory - land that out - shines the sun.

```
/       /       /    /       A7        /   Dm  /
```
I've got a home in glory - land that out - shines   the sun,

```
F  /    C7 /    F  //
```
'Way   be - yond   the blue.

Chorus:
```
F       /  /     /  /    /          / F7
```
Do, Lord O do, Lord, O do re - mem - ber me,
(O Lordy)
```
B♭      /  /     /  /    /         F  /
```
Do, Lord O do, Lord, O do re - mem - ber me,
(Hallelujah)
```
/       /  /     /  A7      /         Dm  /
```
Do, Lord O do, Lord, O do re - mem - ber me,

```
F  /    C7 /    F B♭ F
```
'Way   be - yond   the blue.

Joshua Fought the Battle of Jerico

Dm   /   /   / **Gm** / **A7** / **Dm**   /   / /
Joshua fought the battle of Jeri - co, Jeri - co, Jeri - co, Joshua fought the battle of Jeri - co

    A7   /   **Dm** /   **Dm**   / **A7**   /
And the walls came tumb - ling down.   You may talk about your King of Gi - de - on,

    Dm   / **A7** /   **Dm**   / **A7** /
You may talk about your man of Saul. There's none like good old Joshua,

   A7   / **Dm A7 Dm**   /   / / **Gm** / **A7** /
At the battle of Jeri - co. Yes, Joshua fought the battle of Jeri - co, Jeri - co, Jeri - co,

Dm   /   / /   **A7**   /   **Dm**
Joshua fought the battle of Jeri - co, And the walls came tumb - ling down.

Lonesome Valley

Bb **F** **/ /**   /   **Dm /** / / **F /** / /   **C /** / **C7**
Jesus walked - this lonesome valley, He had to walk - it by him - self - oh,

F7   **/ /**   / **Bb** **/ /** /   **F** / **Bb** /   **F /** /
Nobody else - could walk it for him, He had to walk - it by - him-self.

2. We must walk - this lonesome valley, We have to walk - it by ourselves - oh, -
Nobody else - can walk it for us - We have to walk - it by - ourselves.

3. You must go - and stand your trial, You have to stand - it for yourself - oh,
Nobody else - can stand it for you, You have to stand - it for yourself.

Poor Wayfaring Stranger

     Dm / /   /   /   **/ /** /   **Gm / /** /   **A7 / /**
I'm just a poor   way - faring stranger, A - traveling through this world of woe

  Dm   **/ / /**   /   / **/ /** /   **Gm / /** / **Dm / /**
And there's no sick - ness, toil nor danger, In that bright land to which I go.

   /   **Bb / /** **C**   **F / /** /   **Dm / /** /   **A7 / /**
I'm go - ing there to see my father, I'm go - ing there no more to roam;

  Dm **/ / /**   **A7 Dm / /**   / **Gm / /** / **Dm** **/ /**
I'm just a-go - ing over Jordan, I'm only go - ing over home.

Swing Low, Sweet Chariot

```
 F        /      B♭   C7  F              Am           Gm  C7
Swing low,  sweet char - i - ot, Com - in' for to car - ry me home;
```

```
        F  F7        B♭     C7  Dm     G7     F     C7   F    /
Swing low,   sweet char - i - ot, Com - in' for to car - ry me home.
```

```
    /          /        B♭      C7    F              Am           Gm  C7
I looked over Jor - dan and what did I see, Com - in' for to car - ry me home?
```

```
      F   F7        B♭          C7  Dm     G7     F     C7   F    /
A band of an - gels com - in' after me, Com - in' for to car - ry me home.
```

```
    /       /       B♭     C7   F              Am           Gm   C7
Swing low,  sweet char - i - ot, Com - in' for to car - ry me home;
```

```
   F        F7        B♭      C7  Dm     G7     F     C7   F    /
Swing low,   sweet char - i - ot, Com - in' for to car - ry me home.
```

Nobody Knows the Trouble I've Seen

```
 F         B♭        F        /     /         B♭        C        /
No - bod - y knows the trou - ble I've seen, No - bod - y knows but Je - sus,
```

```
 F         B♭        F      A7 Dm  F     C7       B♭     F
No - bod - y knows the trou - ble I've seen, Glo - ry Hal - le - lu - jah! *Fine*
```

```
         F     /        /      Dm   F  /  C
Some - times I'm up, some - times I'm down: Oh, yes, Lord!
```

```
         F     /      F7    B♭    F  C7   F
Some - times I'm al - most to the ground. Oh, yes, Lord! *D.C. al Fine*
```

Steal Away

```
  C  /   // Am /   //  C  /    /  F G  C //
Steal a - way, steal a - way, Steal  a - way to Je - sus!
```

```
  /  /    //  Am      C  (Em)  /
Steal  a - way, steal a - way home;
```

```
  F   /   C  /  G7  C
I ain't got long  to stay here.
```

Go Down Moses

Dm   / Gm / Dm /   /   /   Dm / B♭   / Dm   A7 Dm /
Go down,   Moses,   way down in Egypt land, Tell ol' Pharoah   let my people go.

        Dm A7   Dm /   /   A7 Dm /
When Israel was in Egypt land, Let my people go.

     /   A7   Dm   /   /   A7 Dm /
Op - pressed so hard they could not stand, Let my people go.

/   / Gm / Dm /   /   /   /   / B♭   / Dm   A7 Dm /
Go down,   Moses,   way down in Egypt land; Tell ol' Pharoah   let my people go.

The Gospel Train
(Get on Board, Little Children)

    F   /   /   /   /   /   C7 /
The gospel train is coming, I hear it close at hand,

    F   /   B♭   /   F   C7   F
I hear the wheels a - rumbling, And rolling through the land.

Chorus :
F7   B♭ /   /   /   F /   /
Get on board, little children, Get on board, little children,

/   B♭ /   /   /   F   C7   F
Get on board, little children, There's room for many a more.

All God's Chillun Got Wings

F   /   /   / /   /   / / /   /   B♭   /
I got a robe, you got a robe. All God's chillun got a robe. When I get to Heav'n I'm goin' to put on my robe,

        F   B♭   F   / C7 /F / /   /   B♭   /
I'm goin' to shout all over God's Heav'n, Heav'n, Heav'n, Ev'rybody talkin' 'bout Heav'n ain't goin' there;

F   / C7 /   F   B♭   F
Heav'n, Heav'n, I'm goin' to shout all over God's Heav'n.

2. I got wings, etc.
3. I got a harp, etc.
4. I got shoes, etc.

My Lord, What a Mornin'

```
F      C7      F      /  /      /      C      /
```
My Lord,   what a morn-in!   My Lord, what a morn-in!

```
F      /  Bb  F    Bb            F      C7      F
```
My Lord! What a morn-in!   When the stars be-gin to fall. *Fine*

```
         F      /    C7 F      /      Bb  F  C7  F    C
```
1. You'll hear the trump-ets sound, To wake all na - tions un - der - ground,

```
F        /    Bb    C7  Dm  Gm      F      Bb  C7  F
```
Look - in' to my God's right hand, When the stars be-gin to fall. *D.C. al Fine*

2. You'll hear the an - gels sing.
3. You'll see my Jes - us come.

Give Me that Old Time Religion

```
D7          G  /      /      /      D7  /      G
```
Give me that old time re - ligion, Give me that old time re - ligion,

```
 /          G7  /      C    /    G    D7      G
```
Give me that old time re - ligion, It's good e -nough for me. (*Fine*)

```
D7    G          /      /      /    D7      /      G
```
 It was good for the Hebrew children, It was good for the Hebrew children,

```
/    G7      /      C      /    G    D7      G
```
It was good for the Hebrew children, And it's good e-nough for me. (*D.C.alFine*)

This Train

```
F      /  /      /      /      /// /      /  /      /    C      ///
```
This train is bound for glo - ry, this train,   This train is bound for glo - ry, this train,

```
F      /  f7      /      Bb  /      /    C7
```
This train is bound for glo - ry, If you ride it, you must be ho- ly,

```
F      /  /      /      /      /
```
This train is bound for glo - ry, this train.

2. This train won't pull no extras, this train, This train won't pull no extras, this train,
This train won't pull no extras, Don't pull nothin' but the midnight special,
This train won't pull no extras, this train.

Jacob's Ladder

| C | / | / | / | G7 | / | / | C |

We are climb - ing Jac - ob's Lad - der, We are climb - ing Jac - ob's Lad - der,

| / | C7 | F | C | / | G7 | C | / |

We are climb - ing Jac - ob's Lad - der, Sol - diers of the Cross.

1. Every rung get higher, higher (3X) Solders of the Cross.
2. Rise, shine, give God glory (3X) Soldiers of the Cross.

Lord, I Want to Be a Christian

| C | / | / | F | / | C | / | / |

Lord, I want to be a Christ - ian, In my heart, In my heart,

| C | / | / | F | / | C | / / |

Lord, I want to be a Christ - ian. In my heart.

Refrain:

| / | F | /// | C | // |

In my heart,   in my heart,

| / | / | / | F | / | C |

Lord, I want to be a Christ - ian, In my heart.

2. Lord, I want to be more loving in my heart. (2X) *Refrain*
3. Lord, I want to be more holy in my heart. (2X) *Refrain*
4. Lord, I want to be like Jesus in my heart. (2X) *Refrain*

Rock-A My Soul

| C | / | / | / | G7 | / | / | / |

Rock - a my soul in the bo - som of A - bra - ham, Rock - a my soul in the bo - som of A - bra - ham,

| C | / | / | / | G7 | / | C | / |

Rock - a my soul in the bo - som of A - bra - ham, ⸘ Oh, rock- a my soul!

| / | / | / | / | / | G7 | C |

When I went down in the val-ley to pray, Oh, rock-a my soul!

| / | / | Am | / | C G7 | C |

My soul got hap - py and I stayed all day, Oh, rock - a my soul! (*Repeat first two lines*)

Ev'ry Time I Feel the Spirit

Chorus:

C7   F   / / /   C   / / F   C   /   / G7   C   //

Ev'ry time I feel the Spir - it,   Movin' in my heart,   I will pray.

C7   F   / / /   C   / / F   C   /   / G7   C   //

Ev'ry time I feel the Spir-it,   Movin' in my heart, I will pray.   *Fine*

       F   C   / /   F   C //   F   C   /   / G7   C   //

1. Up - on the moun - tain, when my Lord spoke, Out of His mouth came fire and smoke;

       F   C   / /   F   C // F   C   / / G7   //

Look'd all a - round me it look'd so fine, Till I ask'd my Lord if all were mine. *D.C. al Fine*

2. Oh, I have sorrows, and I have woe, And I have heartache here below,
But while God leads me I'll never fear, For I am sheltered by His care. *D.C. al Fine*

This Little Light of Mine

F   /   / / /   /   / F7 B♭   /   / / /   / F   /

This little light of mine, I'm gonna let it shine,   This little light of mine, I'm gonna let it shine,

 /   /   / / A7   / Dm /   F   / C7 /   F //

This little light of mine,   I'm gonna let it shine; Let it shine, let it shine, let it shine.

2. Hide it under a bushel. NO! (spoken), I'm gonna let it shine, (3X)
Let it shine, let it shine, let it shine.
3. I've got a home in glory land that outshine the sun, (3X)
Let it shine, let it shine, let it shine.

All Night, All Day

Chorus:

 F / / / F7 / / / /B♭ /   /   /   /   / C7 /

 All night, All   day, An - gels watchin' over me, my Lord;

 F / / / Dm / G7 / F   /   /   C7 F B♭ F

 All night, All   day, An - gels watchin' over me.

  F   B♭ F   / B♭ / /   /   /   / C7 /

1. Day is dying in the west, An - gels watchin' over me, my   Lord;

 F   B♭   F Dm G7 F /   /   C7 F B♭ F

Time to sleep and take my rest, An - gels watchin' over me.   *Chorus*

30

Wade in the Water

Chorus:

Dm Bb   **Dm** / /   **A7**   **Dm**   **A7**
Wade   in the wa - ter, Wade   in the wa - ter, chil - dren,

Dm Bb   **Dm**   / /   /   **C**   **Dm**
Wade   in the wa - ter, God's a - gon - na trou - ble the wa - ter.

   Dm   /   **A7**   **Dm**   /   /   **C**   **Dm**
1. Jor - dan's wa - ter is chil - ly and cold, God's a - gon - na trou - ble the wa - ter,

   /   /   **A7**   **Dm**   /   /   **C**   **Dm**
It chills the bod - y, but lifts up the soul, God's a - gon - na trou - ble the wa - ter. *Chorus*

2. Jordan's water is deep and wide, God's a-gonna trouble the water.
Meet my mother on the other side, God's a-gonna trouble the water. *Chorus*

3. If you get there before I do, God's a-gonna trouble the water.
Tell all of my friends I'm coming, too, God's a-gonna trouble the water. *Chorus*

Sometimes I Feel Like a Motherless Child

Chorus:

   Dm   /   /   /   **Gm**   /   **Dm**   /
Some-times I feel like a mother - less child, Some-times I feel like a mother - less child,

    /   /   /   /   **Bb7 Dm A7**   **Dm**
Some-times I feel like a mother - less child, A long way from home;

   Bb7 Dm A7   **Dm**
A long way from home.

Train is A-comin'

   C   /   **F**   **C**   /   /   /   **G**
Train is a-comin', oh Lord, Train is a-comin', oh Lord,

   C   /   **Am**   /
Train is a - comin', Train is a - comin',

   F   **C**   **F**   **C**
Train is a - comin',   oh Lord.

2. Better get your ticket, oh Lord, etc.
3. Johnny's the conductor, oh Lord, etc.

Mary Had a Baby

```
C          /  F   C   /        / /   G
```
Mary had a baby, My Lord, Mary had a baby, My Lord,

```
 C         /  Am    F   /      / /   C
```
Mary had a baby, Mary had a baby, Mary had a baby, My Lord.

2. What did she name him, My Lord, etc.
3. She named him King Jesus, My Lord, etc.
4. Where was he born, My Lord, etc.
5. Born in a manger, My Lord, etc.

Deep River

```
 C  / F  /   C      Am  Em G7 C  C7 F    Am    /           Dm
```
Deep riv-er, my home is over Jordan;   Deep 'riv-er, Lord, I want to cross over

```
G7  C     /       Am      /   Em /      Am D7  Em /
```
Into camp ground. Oh, don't you want to go   to that gos-pel feast

```
G7  C    C7 F  D7      C G7  E7 Am C  / F    /    C      Am  Em   G7
```
That prom-ised land   where all   is peace?   Deep riv - er, my home is over Jordan;

```
 C   C7 F    A7    D7    G7     /   C    /
```
Deep   riv-er, Lord, I want to cross over Into camp ground.

Oh, Sinner Man

```
Dm  /       /              /   C /      /              /
```
Oh, sinner man, where you gon - na run to; Oh, sinner man, where you gon - na run to;

```
Dm  /       /           /   Dm C    Dm /
```
Oh, sinner man, where you gon-na run to, All on that day!

2. Run to the rock, the rock was a-melting, (*3X*)All on that day!
3. Run to the sea, the sea was a-boiling, (*3X*) All on that day!
4. Run to the moon, the moon was a-bleeding, (*3X*) All on that day!
5. Run to the Lord, Lord won't you hide me? (*3X*) All on that day!
6. Run to the devil, the devil was a-waiting, (*3X*) All on that day!
7. Oh, sinner man, you oughta been a-praying, (*3X*) All on that day!
8. Oh, sinner man, you should have found Jesus; (*3x*) Long before that day.

Were You There ?

```
C    /    /    C7    /    Dm  F  G7  /    C (F C)/    /    Em  G7  C    F  C    /    /    G  (B♭ G7) C
```
Were you there when they cru - ci - fied my Lord?   Were you there when they cru - ci - fied my Lord?   Oh!

```
F       C    / E7   / Am  C7  F    /    /    /    /    C
```
Some - times it caus-es me to Trem - ble, trem - ble, trem - ble.

```
/    F    C    Am   /    Dm  F  G7  /    C    F  C
```
Were you there when they cru- ci - fied my Lord?

2. Were you there when they nailed Him to the cross?
3. Were you there when they laid Him in the tomb?
4. Where you there when He rose up from the tomb?

Go Tell It on the Mountain

```
F / B♭   /       F    / Dm / Gm    /    C7  /    F    /    B♭    C7
```
Go tell it on the moun - tain,   O - ver the hills and ev - 'ry - where,

```
F / B♭   /       F    / Dm  / Gm   /    F  C7  F  //
```
Go tell it on the moun - tain That Je - sus Christ is born.   *Fine*

```
   F       /    /    / C7          B♭  C7  F  /
```
Oh, when I was a sin - ner, I prayed both night and day;

```
   /    /    /    /    G7        /    C7 /
```
I asked the Lord to help me, And He showed me the way. *D.C. al Fine*

One More River

```
   F    /    /    /    /          C7    F
```
Old Noah, once he built the ark, There's one more river to cross;

```
   /    /    /    /          /    C7       F
```
He patched it up with hickory bark, There's one more river to cross.

Chorus:
```
F  B♭  F  /  C7       /    F  /  /  B♭  F  /    C7       /    F
```
One more river, and that's the river of Jor - dan, One more river, there's one more river to cross.

2.The animals went in one by one, There's one more river to cross.
The monkeys bang on a big bass drum, There's one more river to cross. *Chorus*
3.The animals went in two by two, etc. The elephant and the kangaroo, etc. *Chorus*
4.The animals went in three by three, etc. The bear, the flea, and the bumble-bee, etc. *Chorus*
5.The animals went in four by four, etc. He shouted, "Enough!" and he shut the door, etc. *Chorus*

Good News

Chorus:

G   /   /   /   D   / G   /

Good news (good news) chariot's a - comin' Good news (good news) chariot's a - comin'

    /   /   /   C   G   D7   G /

Good news (good news) chariot's a - comin' And I don't want it to leave me be - hind.

    G   /   /   /   G   /   /   /

1. There's a long white robe in the heaven I know, There's a long white robe in the heaven I know,

    G   /   /   /   /   D7   G

There's a long white robe in the heaven I know,   And I don't want it to leave me be - hind. *Chorus*

3. There's a pair of wings in the heaven I know, etc.
4. There's a pair of shoes in the heaven I know, etc.
5. There's a starry crown in the heaven I know, etc.
6. There's a golden harp in the heaven I know, etc.

He's Got the Whole World in His Hands

G7   C / // / / /

He's got the whole world in His hands,

/   G7 / // C / /

He's got the whole world in His hands,

/   / / // / / /

He's got the whole world in His hands,

/   G7 / / / C //

He's got the whole world in His hands.

2. He's got the itty bitty babies in His hands (*repeat three times*)
He's got the whole world in His hands.
3. He's got you and me, brother, in His hands (*repeat three times*)
He's got the whole world in His hands.

Down By the Riverside
(Ain't Gonna Study War No More)

```
        G     /   /     /   /    /   /     /
```
Gon - na lay down my sword and shield ↯ Down by the riv - er - side,

```
D7      /   /     /  G    /   /     /
```
↯ Down by the riv - er - side, ↯ Down by the riv - er - side,

```
        /    /   /     /   /    /   /     /
```
Gon - na lay down my sword and shield ↯ Down by the riv - er - side,

```
   D7   / G DF  G   / G7
```
And study   war no more.

Chorus:
```
  /           C    /   /   /         G    /    /
```
I ain't gon - na stud - y war no more, I ain't gon - na stud - y war no more,

```
  /         D7     / C D7  G / G7   /           C    /    /
```
I ain't gon - na stud - y war no more,   I ain't gon - na stud - y war no more,

```
  /         G    /   /   /             D7   / G D7  G  /  |
```
I ain't gon -na stud - y war no more, I ain't gon - na stud - y   war no more.

2. I'm gonna join hands with everyone, Down by the riverside, down by the riverside,
Down by the riverside. I'm gonna join hands with everyone,
Down by the riverside, And study war no more. *Chorus*

3. I'm gonna put on my long white robe... *Chorus*
4. I'm gonna talk with the Prince of peace... *Chorus*

Hymns of Thanksgiving

Thanksgiving Prayer

```
 C          /      G7         C        G          Am D7 G Am   D7    G
```
We ga - ther to - gether to ask the Lord's blessing, He chastens and hastens His will to make known;

```
   G7     C         G7          C        F          G         C  Dm G7    C
```
The wicked oppressing cease them from dis - tressing, Sing praises to His name, He for - gets not His own.

2. Beside us, to guide us, our God with us joining, Ordaining, maintaining His Kingdom divine;
So from the beginning the fight we were winning; Thou, Lord, was at our side, all glory be Thine.

3. We all do extol Thee, Thou Leader triumphant, And pray that Thou still our Defender wilt be.
Let Thy congregation escape tribulation; The Name be ever praised! O Lord, make us free!

Come, Ye Thankful People, Come

```
 F   /  C    F Dm C  F     /    /  C   F Dm  Gm  A7
```
Come, ye thank - ful, peo - ple, come, Raise the song of har - vest home;

```
 D7 /  Gm  /  C      /  F  / G7 C  Dm C  G7 C
```
All is safe - ly gath - ered in, Ere the win - ter storms be - gin;

```
 /   /  C7  /   F  C7 F   /  /    / F7 B♭ F    B♭
```
God, our Ma - ker, doth pro - vide, For our wants to be sup - plied;

```
 D7 /  Gm  /  C   /  F     B♭  / F / /   C7 F
```
Come to God's own tem - ple, come, Raise the song of har - vest home.

Break Thou the Bread of Life

```
C    /      /     /    /   /     G /C /     /        /        G  D7 G  /
```
Break Thou the bread of life, Dear Lord, to me, As Thou didst break the loaves be - side the sea;

```
G7   /      C    / G D7      G G7 C  /  Dm     /      / G7 C
```
Be - yond the sacred page I seek Thee, Lord,   My spirit pants for Thee, O liv - ing Word.

2. Bless Thou the truth, dear Lord, to me to me, As Thou didst bless the bread by Galilee,
Then shall all bondage cease, all fetters fall; And I shall find my peace, my all in all.

O God, Our Help in Ages Past

C /   F C Am F G C   / Am   C Am D7 G

O God, our help in   a - ges past, Our hope for years to come,

/   C   F   Dm G7 C   F E7   C   F C Dm G7 C F   C

Our shel - ter from the storm - y blast And our e - ter - nal home!

We Give Thee But Thine Own

C7 F   /   B♭ C7   F   F7   B♭ F Gm B♭ F   C

We give Thee but Thine own, What - e'er the gift may be;

/   F   /   B♭ C7 Dm C   F   F7 B♭ Gm F   C7   F

All that we have is Thine a - lone, A trust, O Lord, from Thee.

We Plow the Fields

G   /   /   /   D7 G   D7 G   D

We plow the fields, and scat - ter The good seed on the land,

G D A7 D G A7 D   /   Em   A7   D

But it is fed and wa - tered, By God's al - mighty hand;

D7   G   D7 /   G   /   D   /

He sends the snow in win - ter, The warmth to swell the grain,

G   /   C   Em   Am   D7   G

The breez - es and the sun - shine, And soft re - fresh - ing rain.

Refrain:

G   /   D /   G   /   D   /

All good gifts a - round us, Are sent from heav'n a - bove;

G   D G   B7 Em B7 Em G Am / G D7 G

Then thank the Lord, O thank the Lord, For all   His love.

Bless Thou the Gifts

C7   F   A7 Dm Gm C7   /   F   /   B♭ C7 Dm G7 C   G7   C

Bless Thou the gifts our hands have brought, Bless Thou the work our hands have planned

C7 F A7 Dm Gm C7   /   F   /   B♭ C7 F Gm F C7   F

Our is the faith, the will, the thought, The rest, O God, is in Thy Hand.

37

Hymns of Easter and Lent

Christ the Lord is Risen Today

```
  C   /   G   /   F   /   FC  //FC  /GC/  F C F  C F  C  /G C/FC  /G C /
```
Christ the Lord is ris-en to - day, Hal - le - lu - jah! Sons of men and an - gels say, Hal - le - lu - jah!

```
 G    D7  G  G7 C   G7    C  / G/D7 G /D7 G / /   G7 C        /  F   /FC //F / C G7 G
```
Raise your joys and tri - umphs high,   Hal - le - lu - jah! Sing, ye heav-ens, and earth re-ply, Hal - le -lu - jah!

Abide with Me

```
C G7  /  Am   C F  C G G7 C  /  F    C    F    C  Dm  G   C  D7  G  G7
```
A - bide with me! Fast falls the even - tide, The dark - ness deep - ens, Lord with me   a - bide!

```
  C   G7  / Am   C  /  F A7  /  Dm G7  C  G7 C   G7 Am Dm  C   G7 C
```
When oth - er help - ers fail, and com-forts flee; Help of the help - less, Oh,   a - bide with me!

Are Ye Able

```
  F   /  /  //    Bb   / / /   C7  /  /  /   F   //
```
"Are ye a - ble," said the Mas - ter, 'To be cru - ci - fied with Me?"

```
  /      /   / /  /  Bb   / / /    G7  / C  Bb  C7 ///
```
"Yea," the stur - day dream - ers an - swered, "To the death we fol - low Thee."

Refrain:
```
 F  /A7 /   Dm  //F7 Bb / / C7  F   ///C / Bb   C7  F  /  // C/ G7 /   C / C7/
```
Lord, we are a - ble, our spir - its are Thine,   Re - mold them, make us like Thee, di - vine:

```
 F  /A7 /   Dm  //  F7 Bb  // /   A7 // /Gm/ Bb  / F  /Gm /F  Gm F  C7 F
```
Thy guid - ing ra - diance a - bove us shall be   A bea - con to God,   to love and loy -al-ty.

2. "Are ye able?" still the MasterWhispers down eternity,
And heroic spirits answer, Now as then in Galilee: *Refrain*

Hosanna, Loud Hosanna

G / / / C D G /
Ho - sanna, loud ho - san - na The little children sang;

/ / / / C / D7 G /
Through pillared court and tem - ple The lovely an - them rang;

/ / D / G / D /
To Jesus, who had blessed them Close folded to his breast,

G / / / C / D7 G
The children sang their prais - es, The simplest and the best.

2. From Olivet they followed Mid an exultant crowd,
The victor palm branch waving, And chanting clear and loud;
The Lord of men and angels Rode on in lowly state,
Nor scorned that little children Should on His bidding wait.

Beneath the Cross of Jesus

C / / B7 / C / / / G7 / / / C //
Be - neath the cross of Je - sus I fain would take my stand,

E7 Am / / E7 Am A7 Dm Am Dm / F7 / E7 //
The shad - ow of a might - y rock With - in   a wear - y land;

C / / / G7 C G7 C7 / F / A7 / Dm //
A home   with - in the wil - der - ness, A rest up - on the way,

/ G7 / / / C / C7 F C / / G7 C //
From the burn - ing of the noon - tide heat, And the bur - den of the day.

2. Upon the cross of Jesus Mine eye at times can see
The very dying form of One Who suffered there for me;
And from my smitten heart with tears Two wonders I confess,
The wonders of His glorious love And my unworthiness.

39

Nearer My God to Thee

F / C7 Dm B♭ /   // F / / / C /// F / C7 Dm B♭/ //   F/ C7 / F ///
Near - er, my God, to Thee, Near - er to Thee. E'en though it be a Cross that raiseth me,

/ / B♭ / F /   // / / B♭ / F /   C /
Still all my song shall be Near - er my God, to Thee,

F / C7 Dm B♭ /   // F / C7/ F   //
Near - er, my God, to Thee, Near - er to Thee!

Crown Him with Many Crowns

C   Am   F   /   C   G7 C G   /
Crown Him with many crowns, the Lamb up - on His throne;

C   Am   D7   G   C G D7   G /
Hark how the heav'nly anthem drowns all music but its own.

C   C7   F   D7   /   G G7
A - wake my soul and sing of Him who died for thee

C   F C C7   C   F G7   C
And hail Him as thy matchless King through all e - ter - ni - ty.

2. Crown Him the Lord of Life who triumphed o'er the grave
And rose victorious in the strife for those He came to save.
His glories now we sing who died and rose on high,
Who died eternal life to bring and lives that death may die.